Dear Parent:
Your child's love of reading starts here!

Every child learns to read in a different way and at his or her own speed. Some go back and forth between reading levels and read favorite books again and again. Others read through each level in order. You can help your young reader improve and become more confident by encouraging his or her own interests and abilities. From books your child reads with you to the first books he or she reads alone, there are I Can Read Books for every stage of reading:

SHARED READING
Basic language, word repetition, and whimsical illustrations, ideal for sharing with your emergent reader

BEGINNING READING
Short sentences, familiar words, and simple concepts for children eager to read on their own

READING WITH HELP
Engaging stories, longer sentences, and language play for developing readers

READING ALONE
Complex plots, challenging vocabulary, and high-interest topics for the independent reader

ADVANCED READING
Short paragraphs, chapters, and exciting themes for the perfect bridge to chapter books

I Can Read Books have introduced children to the joy of reading since 1957. Featuring award-winning authors and illustrators and a fabulous cast of beloved characters, I Can Read Books set the standard for beginning readers.

A lifetime of discovery begins with the magical words **"I Can Read!"**

Visit www.icanread.com for information
on enriching your child's reading experience.

JUST AN
ADVENTURE AT SEA

GINA MARU

BY MERCER MAYER

WITHDRAWN

HARPER

An Imprint of HarperCollinsPublishers

To Peyton & Wyatt Ongley—
a couple of great critters!

I Can Read Book® is a trademark of HarperCollins Publishers.

www.icanread.com

Library of Congress Control Number: 2016952353
ISBN 978-0-06-243141-7 (trade bdg.) — ISBN 978-0-06-243140-0 (pbk.)

17 18 19 20 21   LSCC   10 9 8 7 6 5 4 3 2 1   ❖   First Edition

A Big Tuna Trading Company, LLC/J. R. Sansevere Book
www.littlecritter.com

Dad buys a boat.

We are going fishing in the ocean.

But first we will fix up the boat.

"We must paint the boat,"
Dad says.
But I say, "Painting is hard."

We give the boat a new name.
"The *Gina Maru* is a good
name," I say.
Dad agrees.

The fishing day is here.

We hook the boat to our car.

We get all our fishing stuff
and off we go!

We buy bait to catch the fish.
"This stuff is nasty!" I say.

Then we drive to the boat ramp
to put our boat in the water.

Dad forgets to put the drain plug
in the bottom of the boat.

It fills with water and sinks.
We have to pull it out and drain it.

Now we are all set to go fishing.

The ocean is calm and smooth.

We bait our hooks

and cast our lines.

Dad puts out more fishing lines.

"Why so many?" I ask.

"To catch more fish," Dad says.

We wait a long time.
The sun is hot, and there
is no breeze.

Dad says, "Look, seagulls. That means fish. Let's go!"

We speed over to the birds.
Sure enough, there are fish . . .
lots of fish, everywhere!

Wham!

All the lines have caught a fish.

We reel them in.

But the lines get tangled,
and all the fish get away.
"What a mess!" I say.

We try to untangle the lines.
That is no fun.

I think the fish are laughing at us.

Dad says, "That is silly!

Fish don't laugh."

"Over there," says Dad.

"Do you see the whales?"

We go for a better look.

The whales are very big.

They are leaping out of the water.

I yell, "Dad, we are too close!"

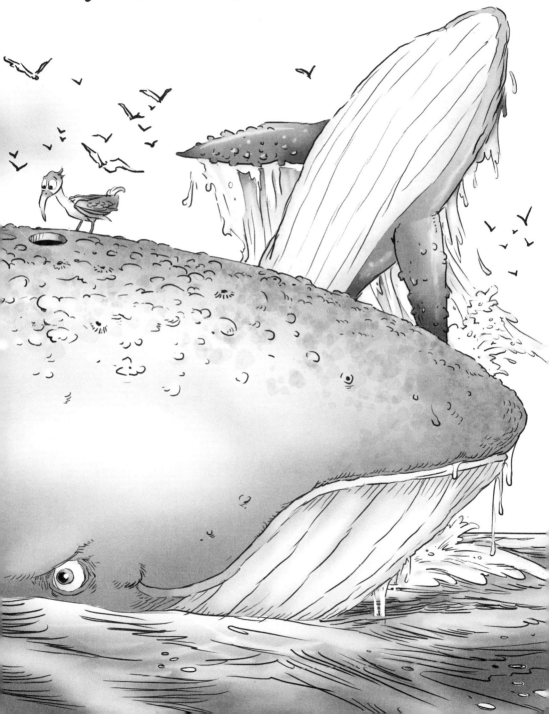

A whale tail shoots up into the air
and comes down with a big splash.
The water floods our boat.

The whales are bored. They leave.
"Look, Dad," I say. "See all
the big fish around the boat?"

Dad looks nervous. He says,
"We have to bail—real quick!
Those fish are sharks!"

"Look at the dolphins, Dad," I say.

"Sharks are afraid of dolphins."

The sharks run.

"That was fun," I say.

But Dad says, "It was just enough adventure for one day."